FOR COLÉ

For Cole

Matt dedicates this book to his childhood and children, Sadie & Greyson—Imagination is the key to endless possibilities throughout this strange and beautiful journey we call life!

A special thanks to Karen Torop for her insight, editing, love, and support.

Ashley dedicates this book to her mom, dad, and brother—Thank you for a sweet childhood filled with laughter, imagination, and fresh air!

The Virginia Diversity Foundation dedicates this book to the idea that gaining a deeper understanding of diversity, wellness, and inclusion in the American experience is critical to healing our great, diverse nation and making the world a better place for our children.

www.mascotbooks.com

When I Was Your Age There Were Dragons

For more information, please contact:
Mascot Books, an imprint of Amplify Publishing Group
620 Herndon Parkway, Suite 320
Herndon, VA 20170
info@mascotbooks.com

Library of Congress Control Number: 2022905691

CPSIA Code: PRV0722A

ISBN-13: 978-1-63755-507-1

Printed in the United States

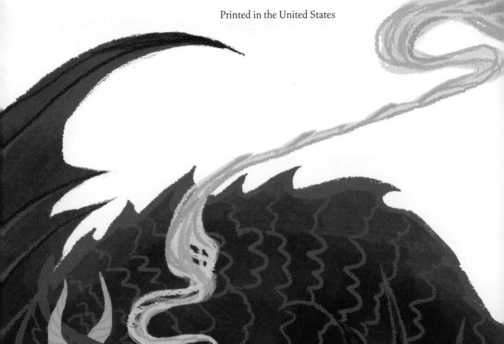

Let me tell you a story...
Once upon a time, when I was your age,
All we wanted to do was play and play,
Outside all through the day,

Until our parents called to say:

"Come inside, kids, it's getting late!"

So we trudged indoors with grass stains on our shirts
and leaves in our hair, knees covered with dirt.

Of course we all sat down for dinner,
because children need to eat.
We must have the strength to send our enemies to defeat!

For then we'd pretend we were defenders of our forts,
Built with pillows and blankets, with flags made of shorts.

Our flagpoles were broomsticks.
We waved cardboard swords.
Stuffed animals manned the ramparts
and fought off the hordes.

At last, when it was finally time for bed,
Oh, the books we read and read!

With flashlights under covers after
Mother turned out the lights,
And Father said: "You need to go to sleep now.
𝕲𝖔𝖔𝖉𝖓𝖎𝖌𝖍𝖙!"

We'd dream of new adventures in far-off ᴅistant ᴌanᴅs,

Off they set through fields of green,
into the fading light of the evening,

And plan how we'd travel there
with our **merry** little band.

Through forests where fairies tended ancient groves of mighty oak trees.

We'd climb over misty mountains

And sail through night and day.
Oh, the 𝖜𝖎𝖑𝖉 things we'd see!

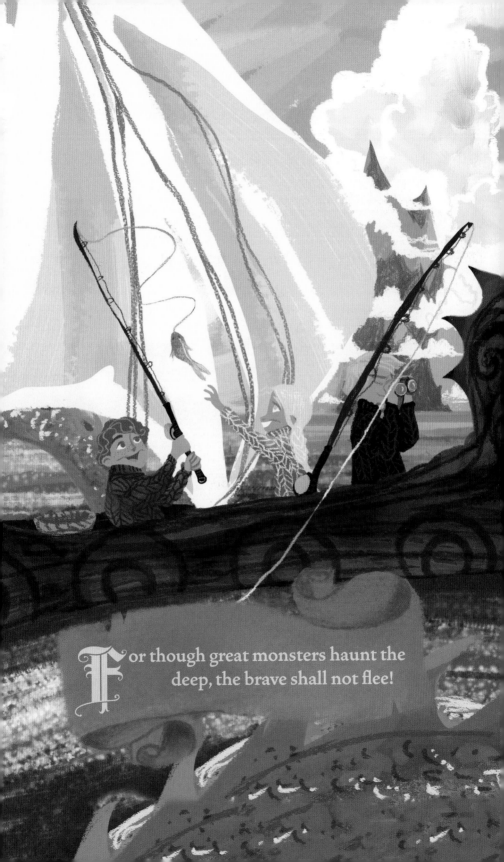

For though great monsters haunt the deep, the brave shall not flee!

thousand years and more, the dwarves had mined gold from the hills by the sea, carving elaborate dragons into the cliffs to scare away thieves.

The doughty knight dismounted his trusty steed to face the fire the Dragon King breathed.

When I was *your* age there were *dragons!*

And **magicians,**

"Tell me," said the mage, "what it is you seek. Fame, fortune, and glory? Then look to the East!"

"Sit we down now to eat," cackled the witch with glee. "I hope you're as hungry as me!"

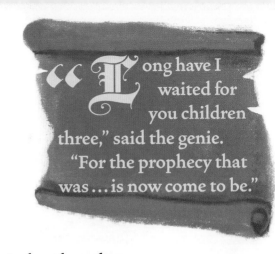

"Long have I waited for you children three," said the genie. "For the prophecy that was ... is now come to be."

And genies in bottles who granted three wishes!

But only if we washed the dishes and cleaned our rooms,
Picked up the pillows and put away the brooms,

Took the dog for a walk and fed the cat,

Finished our homework,

and washed off in the bath.

No talking in class, no chewing gum, please stand in line. Raise your hand if you know the answer, and if you don't that's fine.

When I was your age, there was
sooo much snow in winter.

And summer was *forever.*

It *always* rained in April.

And September changed the weather.

When I was your age, the years passed,
slow as molasses.

Every day lasted a lifetime, filled with fun and laughter!

When the world is full of wonder, the stories never end.
Your imagination runs wild, especially when you pretend

You're a pirate on the high seas in search
of Treasure Island!

Or a daredevil explorer,

or an astronaut,

or a pilot,

flying a spaceship

way into outer space!

In search of distant places

before returning to
your base.

For though the day may be done, the fun lives
on and on...

You simply need a stick and you'll have a **magic wand!**

I have grown up now, but my stories are not gone.

They are here for you, my child, for your days are *looong*.

You have so many possibilities, you'll see.
There are so many games you'll play, so many
books you'll read!

One day when you sit here with your own stories to tell,
About how the Wild West was won and kingdoms rose
and fell,

You'll remember the days when you couldn't
wait to play and play.

And you'll smile when you call and say:
"Come inside, kids, it's getting late!"

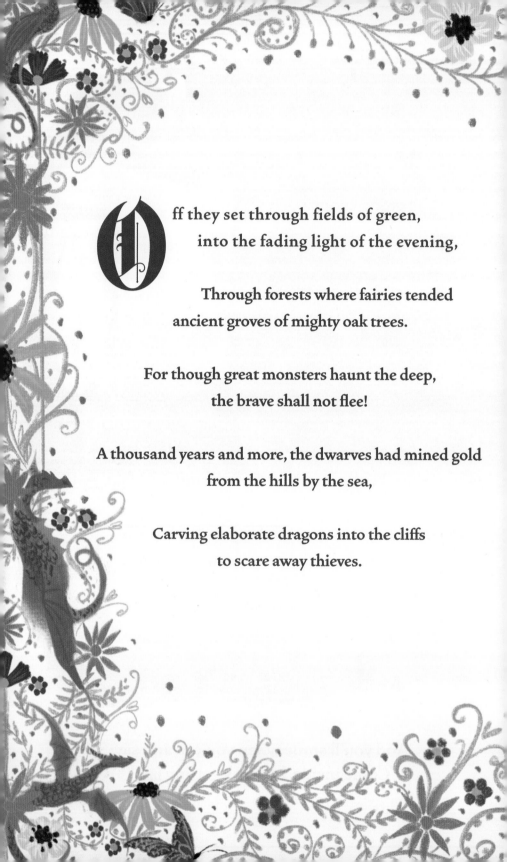

Off they set through fields of green,
into the fading light of the evening,

Through forests where fairies tended
ancient groves of mighty oak trees.

For though great monsters haunt the deep,
the brave shall not flee!

A thousand years and more, the dwarves had mined gold
from the hills by the sea,

Carving elaborate dragons into the cliffs
to scare away thieves.

The doughty knight dismounted his trusty steed
to face the fire the Dragon King breathed.

"Tell me," said the mage, "what it is you seek.
Fame, fortune, and glory? Then look to the East!"

"Sit we down now to eat," cackled the witch with glee.
"I hope you're as hungry as me!"

"Long have I waited for you children three," said the genie.
"For the prophecy that was ... is now come to be."

About the Author

Matthew E. "Matt" Bass is, among other things (including lawyer, sportsman, and musician), a writer, and author. He is also proud daddy to daughter Sadie and son Greyson, and husband to wife Kelbi. The Bass family lives in Matt's hometown of Berryville, Virginia. Matt has long been a fan of fantasy literature and cinema, spurred by early memories of his father reading him and his brother *The Hobbit* and The Lord of the Rings trilogy by the inimitable J.R.R. Tolkien. Matt met Ashley by chance when she accidentally sent him a beautifully illustrated Christmas card meant for a neighbor. After seeing some of Ashley's artwork and working with her on *In Mommy's Tummy,* Matt knew he had a great excuse to write a book filled with fantasy-driven artwork, and thus *When I Was Your Age There Were Dragons* was conceptualized and brought to life.

Other children's books by Matt Bass include: *In Mommy's Tummy* (also with Ashley Bittner), as well as *Your Shoes Do Not Fit Me* and *My Coat Is Too Big!* (with Danny Mitchell).

All are available online at www.matthewbassbooks.com.

About the Illustrator

Ashley Bittner spent her childhood in coastal California, and her adult years in Northern Virginia. She has a love for both the seashore and the countryside. Her inspiration for the artwork in this book stems from old fairy tales and nostalgic memories of her childhood, the whimsical cottages of Virginia, along with the deep woods, rolling hills, and fields of flowers native to her county. Ashley started drawing at the age of five, and has pursued art classes at her local college, and also studied under accomplished art masters. Along with her work in freelance illustration, her hobbies include decorating, arranging flowers, gardening, and working with horses.